This book belongs to

_____

Published by Advance Publishers
© 1998 Disney Enterprises, Inc.
All rights reserved. Printed in the United States.
No part of this book may be reproduced or copied in any form
without the written permission of the copyright owner.

Written by Lisa Ann Marsoli
Illustrated by Kevin Kidney, Stacia Martin, Yakovetic, and Kerne Erickson
Produced by Bumpy Slide Books

ISBN: 1-57973-013-2

10 9 8 7 6 5 4 3 2 1

Today was Alice's birthday, and she had a
feeling something special might happen. Her
sister had asked Alice to meet her at the gazebo
near the boathouse at twelve o'clock sharp.

"I wonder if she has a birthday surprise for me," she said to her cat, Dinah. The cat looked up from its cozy spot on the bed and meowed. "What do you mean, you're not telling?" Alice laughed as she sat down next to her pet and began to stroke its fur.

Suddenly there was a knock on Alice's bedroom door. "Is that you, sister?" Alice asked, rising from the bed. "I can't possibly be late. It's only eleven o'clock." And as Alice opened the door, she cast a quick glance at the clock on her nightstand to check the time.

"Ah, but you are late! You are late! For a very important date!" said the White Rabbit, who stood on the threshold. He took out his pocket watch and shook his head in dismay. "Well, don't just stand there!" he told Alice. "Follow me!"

Now, Alice had followed that White Rabbit once before and ended up in a place called Wonderland. It was a place where anything could happen, and not all of it pleasant. Still, Alice did love a good adventure — and she had a whole hour until she had to meet her sister.

"Mr. Rabbit!" Alice called as the White Rabbit raced down the hall and started up the stairs to the attic. "Wait for me!"

Alice took the stairs two at a time, trying to keep up. "Go on!" urged the flowers on the wallpaper, their petals waving hello. "You can do it!"

Alice nearly fell over in surprise and had to grab the railing to steady herself. "Oh, my goodness!" she exclaimed. "It's been a long time since I've been up here — but I don't remember it looking like this at all!"

"Do hurry!" cried the White Rabbit from the top of the stairs. "The tea is getting cold!"

When Alice reached the attic, she found the Mad Hatter and the White Rabbit standing at a large table. "So good of you to come!" welcomed the Mad Hatter. "We'll just set another place!" And with that, a cup and saucer jumped out of a box and onto the table.

"What kind of a party is this?" asked Alice.

"Why, an un-birthday party, of course," the Mad Hatter replied.

"But today *is* someone's birthday," explained Alice. "Mine!"

"Then you'll have to leave," the Mad Hatter said crossly, pointing to the window.

"But I can't fly," Alice protested.

"Time to be going!" said the White Rabbit, ignoring her. Then he took Alice's hand and pulled her out the window after him.

Outside, the White Rabbit's umbrella billowed open. As they drifted to the ground, Alice wondered, "Why didn't we just take the stairs?"

When they had landed, Alice looked around, bewildered. She found herself in a garden — but one unlike any she had ever seen before. Lollipops sprang from the ground like flowers. Bushes hung

heavy with cupcakes, and the stepping stones were chocolate cookies.

"What is this place?" she asked. But the White Rabbit had disappeared.

Alice was getting hungry, so she plucked a lemon cupcake from a bush and took a bite. Then she noticed that the lollipop flowers were towering over her. "Oh, no!" Alice moaned. "I've shrunk!"

Just then the Dodo Bird came strolling through the garden of treats. "What is that little squeaking sound?" he wondered out loud.

"It's me!" shouted Alice as loudly as she could.

"Did you say something?" the Dodo asked, bending down to address a caterpillar inching across the ground.

"No, I did!" Alice screamed.

The Dodo pulled a magnifying glass out of his jacket pocket and got down on his knees for a closer look. When he did, Alice explained how she had eaten the cupcake and shrunk. "Well, it serves you right," said the Dodo. "It's pests like you that ruin nice gardens. I told the White Rabbit to put a fence around this one!" And then he ambled off, mumbling to himself and shaking his head.

Alice began walking, looking up to make sure no one came along and stepped on her. She didn't see the enormous ant hole until it was too late.

"Ooooooh!" cried Alice as she fell down, down, down into the dark.

When Alice stopped falling, she was sitting in a tunnel. "Which way should I go?" she wondered. Then she heard something ticking very softly in the distance. She decided to follow the noise, and as she did, it got louder and louder. "Tick-tock, tick-tock," the noise echoed.

Finally, Alice saw what looked like the mouth of a cave up ahead. She walked through it and found the White Rabbit standing in a room filled with all shapes and sizes of clocks.

"Well, it's about time, indeed!" sputtered the Rabbit. "You're very, very late!"

"Oh, no!" remembered Alice. "I am very late! I was supposed to meet my sister at noon — and now look at the time!" All the clock faces in the room showed one o'clock.

"Come along, then!" the White Rabbit instructed her. Then he jumped through a hole in the ceiling. But Alice was much too small to jump that high.

"Help!" she called. "Someone get me out of here!"
Moments later, rain began to shower down from
the hole in the ceiling. When it fell on Alice, she
began to grow, just like a flower. She got taller and
taller until her head popped out of the ground. When
she had finished growing, Alice stepped out of the
hole and brushed the dirt from her head.

Before her stood two little round men who
looked exactly alike.

"Tweedledee and Tweedledum, at your service!"
they exclaimed, bowing before her.

"Do you know how I can get to the gazebo?"
Alice asked. "It's my birthday and —"

"Your birthday!" interrupted Tweedledee. "Why,
you must let us recite a special birthday poem!"

"Let me choose!" shouted Tweedledum, pulling
a piece of paper from his pocket.

"No, me!" Tweedledee insisted, waving another.

"Really, I don't have time right now," Alice
tried to explain, but the twin brothers wouldn't listen.
They continued to argue, taking poems out of what
seemed like hundreds of pockets.

Alice walked away, shaking her head. Clearly
these two wouldn't be of any help.

"But you might!" Alice exclaimed, thinking that
she spotted her cat Dinah in a tree.

Getting closer, Alice saw that the creature wasn't her pet at all. It was the Cheshire Cat. He grinned an enormous grin and pointed.

"Is that the way to the gazebo?" asked Alice. But instead of answering, the cat disappeared.

Alice wandered along through the forest until she saw a clearing up ahead. Just as she emerged from the trees, someone yelled, "Duck!" Alice did as she was told. To her surprise, a hedgehog whizzed by her head.

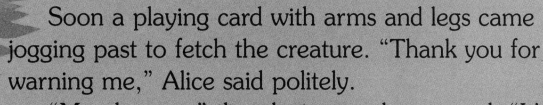

Soon a playing card with arms and legs came jogging past to fetch the creature. "Thank you for warning me," Alice said politely.

"My pleasure," the playing card answered. "It's always dangerous when the Queen plays croquet!"

Looking to the field beyond, Alice saw an enormous table in the grass. At the table sat the Queen of Hearts, her husband the King, the White Rabbit, and other guests.

"There you are!" bellowed the Queen of Hearts, looking straight at Alice. "Come here at once!"

"Yes?" Alice asked timidly.

"How dare you keep me waiting!" the Queen shouted angrily.

"I'm terribly sorry," apologized Alice. "I didn't even know I was invited." Then she sat down at an empty place at the table.

"Invited!" shrieked the Queen. "I should say not!"

"You're supposed to be serving the food," the King whispered.

"There must be some mistake!" protested Alice.

"No one disobeys the Queen!" the Queen cried, outraged. "Guards! Off with her head!"

Alice sprang from the table. She knew that the Queen must have her confused with someone else, but she decided now was not the time to argue.

"That's better!" said the Queen. "Now bring us some strawberries!"

Alice went over to a buffet table laden with food, brought the bowl of strawberries, and ladled some onto each guest's plate.

"Now the tomatoes!" commanded the Queen. Next she ordered Alice to bring them cherries, then cranberries, then raspberries. This was the Queen's annual Red Banquet, and all the food served had to be red, of course.

Back and forth, back and forth Alice went to the table. After the raspberries, she had to bring everyone tarts with red icing and red fruit punch.

At last, tired of the Queen's orders, Alice stood and faced her.

"If you want one more thing, you'll have to get it yourself!" the girl announced.

The Queen of Hearts leapt from her chair, and
Alice jumped backward in fright. She tripped over the
Queen's croquet mallets and went sailing into the
air. Up she went into the clear blue sky, where she
bounced from cloud to cloud.

Her last bounce sent her soaring straight through an open window. When she hit the floor, she realized she was in her very own bedroom! Alice looked at her rumpled bed, then at her clock, and realized she must have fallen asleep.

"Why must I always dream of that silly White Rabbit?" Alice asked Dinah, who was still curled up on the bed.

Then Alice remembered she was supposed to meet her sister. She raced down the stairs and out of the house to the gazebo. Just as she was arriving, she saw a group of her friends getting ready to leave.

"Alice!" exclaimed her sister. "You almost missed your own birthday party!"

"I'm so sorry," Alice apologized. "I guess I fell asleep and lost track of the time."

"Well, don't worry. You won't ever be late again!" her sister said, smiling. When Alice looked confused, her sister handed her a gaily wrapped box.

"What is it?" Alice asked, shaking the package.

"Open it," her sister said.

Alice tore through the paper and lifted the lid.

Inside was a tiny alarm clock on a chain.

"Oh, thank you! It's beautiful!" cried Alice. "What time is it? I'm going to set it right now."

Her sister went back to the gazebo and came out carrying Alice's favorite dessert. "Time for cake!" she exclaimed.

Alice met a rabbit
Who kept her on the run.
She thought that if she followed him,
She just might have some fun.
Instead of falling fast asleep,
She should have watched the clock.
Now she always knows the time,
'Cause her necklace goes tick-tock!